THE COST
OF COOL

KLASKY CSUPO INC.

Based on the TV series *Nickelodeon Rocket Power*™
created by Klasky Csupo, Inc. as seen on Nickelodeon®

SIMON SPOTLIGHT
An imprint of Simon & Schuster Children's Publishing Division
1230 Avenue of the Americas, New York, New York 10020

Manufactured in the United States of America

First Edition

4 6 8 10 9 7 5

ISBN 0-689-84588-X

Library of Congress Catalog Card Number: 2001095195

THE COST
OF COOL

by Adam Beechen

illustrated by Fran Talbot
and Juliet Newmarch

Simon Spotlight/Nickelodeon

New York   London   Toronto   Sydney   Singapore

chapter 1

"Here they come!" Sam Dullard shouted excitedly. He hopped off his bike, took off his helmet, and straightened his glasses, wanting to look his best.

Otto Rocket braked his skateboard to a stop and looked up. His best bud, Twister Rodriguez, did the same. Otto's older sister, Reggie, made a graceful spin on her in-line skates, stopping beside them, and looked down the crowded boardwalk of Ocean Shores.

Otto made a face when he saw what Sam was looking at. "Come on, Sam," he said. "Why are you so interested in them?"

"Yeah, Squid," Twister chimed in. "I think they're creepy!"

"Creepy?" Sam replied in disbelief, smoothing his shirt. "They're cool!"

Down the boardwalk Reggie could see the Scrunchies approaching on their in-line skates. The four girls—Sandi, Mandi, Randi, and Candi—were all thirteen, best friends, and the defending Ocean Shores In-Line Team Competition relay champions. They were called the Scrunchies because they all wore their hair in ponytails held in place with matching scrunchies. The girls were popular to the max—practically every girl Reggie knew wanted to be a Scrunchie.

Twister grimaced. "They walk alike, they talk alike . . . they're like that movie we saw the other night, The Zombie Queens of Planet Gorbleck."

"I bet they're nice," Sam said, climbing back onto his bicycle. "I mean, they're popular for a reason, right?"

"Well, gosh, Sammy," teased Otto, "it sounds like you've got a major crush on the Scrunchies!"

"Lay off, Otto," Reggie warned.

Sam blushed, looking over his shoulder. The Scrunchies wove their way gracefully through the crowd, headed toward them. "M-Me? A c-crush? I don't think so!"

"Don't worry, Squid-man, we think it's sweet," Twister said with a grin, putting his hand on the back of Sam's bike. "Now go say hi to your girlfriends!" He gave the bike a shove, sending him pedaling wildly into the crowd.

"Whoa!" Sam yelled as he tried to gain control of his bike. Everyone on the boardwalk ran out of the way.

Reggie scowled. "Twister, you dork!" She pushed off on her skates toward Sam.

As Reggie darted through the crowd, she saw that Sam's wobbly bike ride was taking him straight toward the oncoming Scrunchies. Driving hard for extra speed, Reggie spun around two old ladies, and jumped over a three-wheeled baby carriage. She quickly caught up with Sam, grabbing his bike by the handlebars and pulling him out of the way just before he could smack into the girls.

They both fell into a pile of cardboard boxes. "Thanks, Reg," Sam huffed.

"No sweat, Sammy," Reggie puffed.

"Totally rad save," said a voice above them.

"Yeah, mega," said another.

Reggie and Sam looked up and saw the Scrunchies standing over them. They each

wore pink T-shirts with their names in glittery silver letters across the middle.

Mandi smiled. "You're Reggie Rocket, right? Excellent skating!"

"*Way* impressive," Sandi said, nodding seriously, then stooped to pick a piece of cardboard off Sam's shoulder. Sam looked like he was about to faint.

"Uh, thanks," said Reggie, brushing herself off.

"We'll *definitely* see you around," Candi said, as the girls skated away.

Otto and Twister rolled up a second later. "I'm really sorry, Squid," Twister said. "I was only goofing. Are you okay?"

Sam sank back into the boxes, closed his eyes, and smiled. "Am I okay? One of the Scrunchies actually *touched* me!"

chapter 2

"It wasn't a big deal," Reggie said later at the Shore Shack as her father, Ray, set down a huge plate of nachos in front of the kids.

Sam was still smiling. "It was too, Reggie! They thought you were a really good skater! And if the Scrunchies like you, then you're really in!" He elbowed Twister next to him. "And one of them *touched* me!"

Twister rolled his eyes. "We *know*, Squid!" He turned to Reggie. "Reg, promise us you're not going to become a Scrunchie. It'd be totally rank if you turned into a zombie!" He crossed his eyes and stuck his arms out in front of him. "Must. Dress. Like. Everyone. Else," he said in a robotlike voice.

"You wouldn't really ditch us for the Scrunchies, would you, sis?" Otto asked through a mouthful of nachos. "Hanging around with us has got to be more fun."

"Everyone just chill," Reggie ordered. "First of all, the Scrunchies have said, like, two words to me, ever. Second, they're older than me, and the Scrunchies never let in anyone who isn't their age. Third, pass the salsa."

Ray came back to the table and took a seat. So did his friend, Tito Makani. "Who are the Scrunchies, kiddo?" Ray asked.

"They're just a bunch of really popular girls who are totally awesome skaters,"

Reggie explained to her dad. "The guys think the Scrunchies want me to be their next member, but I don't think so."

Ray sat back and scratched his chin, smiling. "Ah, I remember when I was your age, and I got asked to join the North Shore Surfmaster Club. What an honor! They were the coolest of the cool in Ocean Shores, and all I had to do to get in was ride one of the humongous waves at Sandpaper Reef."

Otto's eyes widened. "The beach with all the really sharp coral? Wicked!"

"Did you score, Raymundo?" Twister wanted to know.

"Well, I, uh . . . I considered all my uh, options . . . ," Ray slowly replied. "I weighed the pros and cons—"

"And he chickened out," Tito finished.

"Hey," Ray said defensively, "have you ever seen that coral? I wanted to be a

Surfmaster, but I *really* wanted to stay alive so I could keep surfing! The whole experience taught me a valuable lesson."

Tito nodded. "Like the Ancient Hawaiians say, 'Sometimes the poi at the luau isn't worth the price of admission.'" He looked at Reggie. "Make sure being a Scrunchie is worth it before you pay to get in, little Rocket cuz."

Reggie smiled and shook her head. "Like I said, they haven't even asked me."

"Hey, Reggie," said someone behind her. Everyone turned to look and saw Mandi, Sandi, Candi, and Randi coming up to their table. "The next relay competition is a five-girl event," Mandi told her. "And we liked your skating so much, we want you to be the newest Scrunchie!"

Randi held up a T-shirt. "We even got you one of our shirts!"

Reggie unfolded the pink shirt, which

read, REGGI. Reggie looked back at them, a little awestruck. "I don't know what to say."

"How about, 'Hey, you spelled my name wrong,'" Otto suggested.

"None of *our* names has an *E* at the end," Sandi said, looking at him.

Candi smiled at Reggie. "Think about it and let us know tomorrow. See ya!" They skated out.

Reggie grinned at her friends. "How cool is *that?*"

Sam smiled, but Otto and Twister were not excited. Twister stuck out his arms again. "Must. Wear. Shirt," he said solemnly.

chapter 3

The next day Otto, Twister, and Sam sat in the Rockets' garage, putting on their street hockey gear. Twister shook his head. "Man, I can't believe Reggie's actually thinking about joining the Scrunchies."

Sam struggled to pull on a shin guard. "Maybe you don't know the Scrunchies well enough, Twister," he suggested. "Remember, you hardly knew me when I moved to town, and I turned out to be pretty cool."

Tugging on the padding, Sam lost his balance and crashed onto his back.

Twister rolled his eyes. "Cool as ice, Squid-man—*not*!"

Otto smiled. "Don't worry, guys. I know my big sis. She'd never choose the Scrunchies over Otto-man, the Twistmaster, and Slammin' Sammy!"

Just then Reggie walked into the garage, and the jaws of all three boys dropped to the floor. Reggie was wearing her REGGI T-shirt!

"No way!" Otto shouted, his eyes bugging out.

"Reggie, tell us you're not ditching street hockey practice. You're not ditching *us* for the Scrunchies!" Twister begged.

Reggie shrugged, but didn't look at them. "I'm just going to go say hi and tell them I like the shirt," she said. "I'll meet you guys later."

"What's so great about the Scrunchies anyway?" Otto grumbled.

Reggie sat down on the couch and tried to explain. "Look," she said, "the Scrunchies travel all over for speed-skating tournaments, they're really great skaters, and everyone knows who they are. Think about all the rad people I can meet and places I can go, just from hanging around with them! I'm telling you, I'm not dumping you guys."

Otto shook his head. "I'm telling *you*, sis, there's something about them I don't like."

Reggie stood up again, angry. "Yeah, you're jealous," she said.

Otto pointed to himself in disbelief. "Jealous? Me? Of the Scrunchies?"

Sam shuffled forward in his pads. "Guys—," he started to say before he fell over again.

Otto got in Reggie's face. "Hey, I'm Otto Rocket! I can skate three times as fast as any ponytail-wearing, shirt-matching—"

"Zombie-ized," Twister added helpfully.

"Zombie-ized Scrunchie!" Otto finished. "Why would I be jealous of *them?*"

"Because," Reggie said, turning for the door. "I'm going to go hang with them and not play street hockey with you." And she walked out.

chapter 4

Reggie skated up to Madtown Skate Park, where the Scrunchies liked to practice on the oval speed-skating track.

When Reggie got there, Sandi, Mandi, Candi, and Randi were lacing up their skates and stretching. Their eyes lit up when they saw Reggie wearing her shirt.

"Hey, Reggie," Sandi called out. "Lookin' good!"

Candi skated over to Reggie, followed by the other girls, and tugged on Reggie's sleeve. "It fits great! You were made to be a Scrunchie!"

"Uh, hold on," Reggie said, skating back a few feet. "I just came to tell you I liked the shirt, not to—"

But before she could finish, the Scrunchies swarmed around her.

"Now you just need a few more things so you can really take your place on the team," Mandi said, twirling a scrunchie.

Reggie felt hands tugging at her hair and patting stuff on her face. She was about to scream, but at last the Scrunchies backed away, nodding.

Sandi held out a small makeup mirror to Reggie. Curious, Reggie took it and looked at herself. In the mirror she saw a complete stranger.

She saw someone wearing her hair in a ponytail held by a colorful scrunchie. She saw someone wearing trendy glitter on her

cheeks. "Whoa," Reggie whispered in amazement. "I-I look totally different! I look . . ."

"Cooler," said all four Scrunchies at the same time.

Reggie shrugged, then nodded. "Cooler," she agreed.

The Scrunchies were high-fiving Reggie when Otto, Twister, and Sam skated up, carrying their hockey gear.

For a second, Reggie caught their eyes. She smiled at them, wanting to make peace from their earlier fight. But the boys skated on by, not even recognizing her at first.

Suddenly they all turned, shocked, realizing they were looking at a new Reggie. Otto, Twister, and Sam exchanged looks, then skated toward the hockey oval without saying a word. It was clear they were disappointed.

The Scrunchies hadn't even noticed

them. "Come on," Mandi said. "Let's skate!"

Reggie nodded grimly. "Yeah," she said. "Let's do it."

chapter 5

Otto, Sam, and Twister had started a three-on-three hockey game with Twister's brother Lars, and his friends Pi and Sputz. Otto and his pals were way behind, mostly because Sam was a little distracted.

"Look at them," he said, pulling off his goalie mask and skating out of the goal and over to the edge of the hockey oval, where he looked at the speed-skating track. The Scrunchies were sprinting around it. "Aren't they great skaters?"

"Hey, Sam, keep your mind on the game," Otto shouted, as Pi flattened him with a body check.

"Yeah, Squid," Twister agreed, groaning as his brother got him in a headlock and gave him power noogies. "We could use a little help out here!"

With Otto and Twister both occupied, and Sam out of the Rocket goal, Sputz skated out of his own goal, raced the length of the rink, and scored an easy shot. "Thazzagoalferuss," he drawled.

"That's ten to nothing," Pi cried. "We win!"

The older boys high-fived each other, laughing, as Otto and Twister dusted themselves off. "Man, without Reggie, your team ain't got no Rocket fuel," Lars teased as he skated away with his team.

Otto sighed and stood beside Sam. Twister joined them. "They're right,"

Twister admitted. "We aren't even close to being as good a team as we are with Reggie."

"Reggie hasn't quit our team, and she hasn't quit being our friend," Sam reminded them. "She already has some other friends, like Trish and Sherry. Now she has even more."

Otto watched his sister practice the in-line skating relay with the Scrunchies. She took the baton from Mandi and shot off around the track like a bolt of lightning. Otto saw the smile on Reggie's face as she skated. "I know. But I still don't trust those Scrunchies."

"Reggie will *always* be Reggie," Sam assured him. "She'd never ditch us."

On the track Reggie felt the wind whipping through her ponytail as she skated as fast as she could, clutching the baton tightly. She came around the last turn and saw the Scrunchies there, smiling, urging her to go faster, faster, faster!

A crowd of onlookers had gathered, as they always did when the Scrunchies were practicing. The girls were stars in Ocean Shores—everyone knew who they were. Reggie could hear the crowd chanting, "Go, Scrunchies, go, Scrunchies!" They thought she was one of them—a star! She felt great.

Reggie poured on the speed and crossed the finish line. The crowd cheered! Randi clicked her stopwatch, amazed at what she saw. "That's the fastest time, like, ever!"

"You *go*, girl," Sandi said, high-fiving Reggie.

"You go *fast*, girl," Candi agreed.

"Thanks," Reggie said with a smile, breathing hard.

"You are *this* close to becoming the newest Scrunchie," Mandi said, holding up her thumb and index finger about a half inch apart.

"Really?" Reggie replied. She couldn't help but be excited. "What else do I have to do?" They walked past where Otto, Sam, and Twister were watching them.

"You have to do one more thing," Sandi said mysteriously. "It's the final test. Then you're one of us and there's no looking back!"

"Come on," Candi said, taking Reggie's arm. "We'll tell you about it over mozzarella sticks at the Shore Shack."

"The Shore Shack?" Sam called out. "Hey, Reg, that sounds awesome! We'll meet all of you there, okay?"

Reggie looked at Sam, and started to say, "Sure," then paused and looked at the Scrunchies. They all rolled their eyes, as if to say, "Yeah, right!"

She turned back to Sam. "Maybe I'll just

see you later, guys," Reggie said, skating off with the Scrunchies. She didn't notice the looks of surprise and hurt on the faces of Twister, Otto, and Sam.

chapter 6

Reggie and the Scrunchies sat down at a large round table at the Shore Shack. Reggie looked around nervously for her father. She didn't want him to embarrass her in front of her new, cool friends.

"So, anyway," Mandi continued, "there's a party this weekend, and then we've been invited to two more next weekend. The Scrunchies *always* get invited to the best parties."

"That sounds like fun," Reggie said.

"And we've gone to competitions at Thunder Beach, Speed Land, Mondo Mountain, and Superior Skate Park," Sandi said.

"Superior Skate Park?" Reggie cried in disbelief. "That's in a whole other state!"

"We're the Scrunchies, Reggie," Randi reminded her. "If you join, you'll meet lots of people, go lots of places, and do lots of way rad things."

Hearing them talk about it, Reggie really wanted to be a Scrunchie. She really, really, really wanted it! "That would be so *cool!*" she exclaimed.

"Of course," Sandi said, leaning forward, "that's only if you pass our last test!"

"That's right," Mandi agreed. "You can wear the shirt, and you can skate like lightning, but can you pass our last test?"

Reggie grinned. She couldn't stand it! "Come on, you guys, tell me what it is!"

"For your last test . . . ," Mandi said slowly to draw out the suspense, "for you to become a Scrunchie . . . you have to—"

"Hey!" boomed a voice behind them. "Is that my little girl?"

Reggie looked up as Ray appeared beside the table. "Hi, Dad," she said, hoping he wouldn't do anything goofy.

Ray smiled at everyone. "Hi, ladies! Great day outside, isn't it? Let me get you some menus." He started to walk away, and Reggie exhaled in relief.

But then Ray turned and walked back. "Hey, Reg," he said, "I wanted to get a female opinion. What do you think of these new Bermuda shorts I got today?"

Reggie looked at the shorts quickly. "They rock, Dad."

"Really?" he wondered, fiddling with the waistband. "Because they seem a little loose."

And that's when the shorts fell down to his knees, leaving Ray standing there in his underwear—colorful boxer shorts with red hearts and pink bunnies on them! "Oops," was all Ray could say as he quickly pulled the shorts up and ran toward the counter.

"That's your *dad?*" Randi gasped. The rest of the Scrunchies giggled.

Reggie buried her head in her hands. At least things couldn't get worse.

"Aloha, little Rocket cuz!" called another voice.

Reggie turned and this time saw Tito, wearing a grass skirt! "Oh, no," she said.

"I'm off to teach hula at the community center," Tito explained. "Get a load of these new moves!" He swayed back and forth, his eyes closed dreamily.

"*Mega*-gross," Candi exclaimed, and they all burst into laughter again.

Tito hulaed out the door as Reggie

grinned sheepishly. "My dad and his friend," she said. "They're always goofing with me."

"Well, whatever," Mandi said, brushing off what they had just seen. "Let's talk about your last test."

"Yeah," Reggie agreed. She was ready for anything. Or at least she thought she was.

"For your last test you have to go to Delgado's Drug Store . . ."

"And?" Reggie asked eagerly.

"And you have to steal a scrunchie," Sandi finished.

chapter 7

Reggie played the conversation again in her head for the hundred-millionth time the next morning as she walked around her house to the garage.

"*Steal* a scrunchie?" she had said when Sandi told her what the test was. "Why can't I just buy one? They only cost a quarter!"

Mandi rolled her eyes. "Because then it wouldn't be a *test*, would it? Look, being in the Scrunchies is a big deal, and we don't

let just anybody in. You have to do something *extreme* to show you're cool and to show how bad you want it!"

"Yeah, but stealing . . . ," Reggie responded, unsure.

"Come on, Reggie, it's like you said, scrunchies are cheap," Candi reminded her. "Mr. Delgado won't miss one teeny weenie scrunchie. We all had to do it once."

"Snag a scrunchie," Randi told her, "and it's skating, road trips, loads of new friends, and parties all the way!"

Reggie shook her head, shaking away the memory. She was confused and needed to talk to someone. And Reggie knew she always got the best advice from her friends and family, so she went to the garage.

She saw Twister, Sam, and Otto crashed out on the couches, watching Otto in one of Twister's new skateboarding movies.

"This is my favorite part," Twister said. "Otto goes up for his 540, and look how much sick air he gets! Dude, that's off the meter!"

"Gosh, Otto," Sam said, impressed. "You're practically in the ionosphere!"

"I could have gone higher," Otto said modestly, "but I was worried I might burn up on reentry."

"Hi, guys," Reggie said.

None of the boys looked up.

"I said, hi," she repeated.

"Did you hear something, Twist?" Otto asked.

"*Nada*, Otto-man," his friend answered.

"Okay, I get it," Reggie said. "You're mad because I blew you off a little. But that was only because I was trying to impress the Scrunchies! And now I really need your help."

"You hear something, Squid?" Twister asked Sam.

Sam shook his head. "I don't hear things on the 'cool' frequency," he replied.

"Guys, come on," Reggie pleaded. "I didn't mean anything by it. Look, I need advice, and you're my best friends!"

"Really?" Otto wondered, looking at her at last. "Because you've been acting like we're not your friends. Maybe you should go impress your *new* best friends some more and ask for their advice."

Before Reggie could respond, Otto turned up the volume on the TV. Reggie had no choice but to turn and walk out.

chapter 8

Reggie walked along the street, wondering who else she could talk to. There was no way she could tell her dad she was even thinking about stealing.

Just then her neighbor, Mrs. Stimpleton, called out, "Reggie! Oh, Reggie, yoo-hoo!"

Reggie sighed. Mrs. Stimpleton was nice and all, but Reggie had a lot on her mind today and didn't have time to taste one of Mrs. Stimpleton's strange snacks or hear about her latest crazy hobby.

"Hi, Mrs. Stimpleton," Reggie said, smiling as the older lady bounded toward her. "I'd love to hang out and chat, but I've gotta—"

"Oh, there's always time for friends," Mrs. Stimpleton said cheerfully, wrapping her in a tight hug. Suddenly she broke the hug and looked at Reggie. "Something's bothering you."

Reggie blinked, surprised. How did Mrs. Stimpleton know? "No, Mrs. S, I'm fine."

"Pish-tosh," Mrs. Stimpleton replied. "You can't kid a kidder! Now come inside, have a snack, and tell me all about it!" She took Reggie's arm and marched her toward the house.

🚀 🚀 🚀

"Have another brussel-sprout-on-a-stick, dear," Mrs. Stimpleton said, offering Reggie the tray.

Reggie felt her stomach lurch. "No thanks, I don't want to ruin my appetite for lunch." She stood up from the plastic-covered couch. "Besides, I really should be—"

Mrs. Stimpleton gently pulled her back down. "Not until you tell me what's bothering you."

Reggie looked at her. Mrs. Stimpleton seemed worried about her, like she really wanted to help. "Well," Reggie began, not wanting to tell her the whole truth, "it's not really so much about me as it is, uh, about a *friend* of mine."

Mrs. Stimpleton nodded. "What's the problem with this *friend?*" she asked.

"Well, I, uh, I mean, my friend, has a chance to become really popular and cool, but she has to do something pretty uncool to do it. And she's wondering . . . is it worth it?"

Mrs. Stimpleton smiled. Then she leaned back and yelled, "MERV!"

Mr. Stimpleton came into the room. He didn't look happy, which was pretty normal. "What is it, Violet? I was just about to check the diodes on the automatic pool PH regulator!"

"Tell Reggie about Marvelous Mervy," Mrs. Stimpleton said.

"It's diode time, not storytime!" Mr. Stimpleton huffed, turning to walk out.

"Mervyn J. Stimpleton," Mrs. Stimpleton yelled again, "we have a youngster in trouble here! Now, tell that story!" Mr. Stimpleton slinked back into the room, looking like a puppy that had been scolded for knocking over a chair.

"Who's Marvelous Mervy?" Reggie wanted to know.

"That's what they called me, once upon a time," Mr. Stimpleton said. "I used to be the coolest young person in Ocean Shores," he went on. "Of course, in those days, we said 'swell,' instead of 'cool.'"

"You were cool?" Reggie asked, finding it hard to believe.

"Everyone wanted to hang around with me," Mr. Stimpleton continued. "Adults, kids, boys, girls . . . I dressed in the latest fashions, had all the newest records, and knew the steps to the jitterbug and the lindy hop!"

Reggie shook her head. She couldn't picture it. "What happened?"

"Well, being 'swell' changed," Mr. Stimpleton told her. "Just like that, straw hats and knickers were out, there were new dance crazes, and new music to dance to! Everyone around me suddenly had a new crowd to be with!"

"What did you do?" asked Reggie.

"I kept wearing knickers and straw

hats!" Mr. Stimpleton replied matter-of-factly. "Why waste perfectly good clothes? And I kept dancing the jitterbug! I still do!" He tried to show a few steps, but quickly lost his breath and had to sit down.

"Didn't it bother you that your friends didn't think you were cool anymore?" Reggie asked.

"Bah!" Mr. Stimpleton said with a wave of his hand. "I didn't need those fair-weather fuddy-duddies!"

"The point is," Mrs. Stimpleton explained, "that the things or people that are considered 'cool,' 'swell,' or 'neat-o' change all the time. But who you are doesn't change. Mervy is cool to me for who he is, not for who he hangs around with, what he wears, or how he dances."

She paused for a moment, then added, "Does that help your friend?"

Reggie didn't know how to answer. She

felt more confused than ever. She looked at her watch, then hopped off the couch. "Oh, I gotta jam! Thanks for the snacks, Mr. and Mrs. S!"

She looked back at them as she headed out the door. "And thanks for the advice."

chapter 9

"Do you think we harshed too much on Reggie?" Sam wondered as he sat down on a bench outside the ice-cream parlor. He took a lick of his triple-chocolate cone.

"Squid, much as I hate to say it, Reggie's a zombie now," Twister told him. "I bet she didn't even hear us."

"I don't know, guys," Otto said. "Maybe Sammy's right. Reggie's allowed to have friends besides us, even if we don't like them. It's her choice."

"What do you think we should do?" Sam asked.

"We could start by saying we're sorry," Otto decided.

Twister looked up and saw Reggie on the other side of the street, skating toward Delgado's Drug Store. "Well, here's our chance," he said. The three friends crossed the street.

🚀 🚀 🚀

The bell above the door dinged as Reggie walked into the drugstore. Reggie was so nervous, the sound made her jump.

"Reggie Rocket!" shouted Mr. Delgado with a smile. He was a roly-poly man with a funny mustache. "My favorite customer! Can I help you find something?"

"N-N-No, Mr. Delgado," Reggie answered. "I'm just gonna look around."

"Go right ahead," Mr. Delgado said with a wave. "My store is your store."

Reggie gulped and walked down the aisle to where the Scrunchies were waiting, right in front of the hair care products. Mandi smiled. "Ready to be a Scrunchie, Reggie?"

"I-I guess," Reggie answered nervously, looking around.

"Right on! We'll be down there, looking at magazines while you do the deed," Randi explained. "When you've got it, just walk past us out the store. We'll meet you outside, and then you'll be a Scrunchie!"

The four girls walked toward the front of the store, stopping at the end of the aisle, where they picked up magazines and pretended to look through them. Reggie could see they were keeping an eye on her.

She turned to the racks of scrunchies before her. They came in every color and all of them were small—small enough to easily slip into her pocket. She took a deep

breath and was about to reach out and take one, but then stopped and looked at the other end of the aisle, just to be safe. There was no one there. She could get away with it, no problem.

Reggie looked at the girls waiting for her by the magazines. She heard Randi's voice in her head saying, "Skating, road trips, loads of new friends, and parties all the way!"

She reached out her hand once more. Then she heard Tito's voice in her head urging her, "Make sure being a Scrunchie is worth it."

Reggie stared at the scrunchies for a few more seconds. Finally she walked away down the aisle, past Mandi, Candi, Sandi, and Randi, and out of Delgado's Drug Store.

Reggie stepped out onto the sidewalk, almost bumping into Otto, Twister, and Sam, who were about to come in. A moment later the Scrunchies flew out.

"Reggie, go back!" Randi urged her. "You didn't steal anything!"

"Steal?" Sam gasped.

"Nope," Reggie said to Randi, "and I'm not going to!"

"But you have to," Candi reminded her, "if you want to be one of us!"

"I don't want to be a Scrunchie if I have to do something I know is wrong," Reggie firmly declared.

The Scrunchies were furious. Mandi walked up to Reggie and stood two inches from her nose. "If you don't do this, you'll never be cool! You'll never be a Scrunchie!"

Reggie shrugged, pulling her hair out of its scrunchie, and taking off her REGGI shirt, revealing another shirt underneath. "Maybe not," she said. "But I'll always be a Rocket."

"Way to go, Reg!" Twister shouted happily as Reggie went up to the boys.

"Excellent," Sam agreed, giving her a high five.

Otto held out his fist. "Glad you're back, sis. Sorry about everything I said."

"No sweat, bro," Reggie replied, holding out her fist to give him a knuckle punch. "You were mostly right."

"Sorry you won't get to be in the skating relay," Sam told her.

"That's all right, I'd rather hang with you guys," Reggie answered with a grin. "Hey, think we can get a street hockey rematch with Lars?"

"With you on our team, we'll crush 'em," Otto cheered.

The four of them came together in a huddle. "Game time!" they yelled, then skated away from the Scrunchies toward Madtown. And Reggie never looked back.

About the Author

Adam Beechen lives in Los Angeles and has written many television episodes, books, and comic strips featuring *Rocket Power* and *The Wild Thornberrys*. He has also written scripts for the *Rugrats*, *Little Bill*, and *X-Men* television series.

Adam has never been dared to steal anything, but once, on a dare, he went swimming in a community-center pool after hours. When he was caught, Adam was grounded for a week!